Ho 8/05

D1191373

HOGANSVILLE PUBLIC LIBRARY

Comanche

By

Dave and Pat Sargent

Illustrated by
Jane Lenoir

Ozark Publishing, Inc.
P.O. Box 228
Prairie Grove, AR 72753

Sargent, Dave, 1941-
    Comanche / by Dave and Pat Sargent ; illustrated by Jane
Lenoir. — Prairie Grove, AR : Ozark Publishing, ©2001.
    ix, 36 p. : col. ill. ; 23 cm.   (Saddle-up series)

    "Perseverance"—Cover.
    SUMMARY: The only survivor of Custer's Last Stand, a
courageous red bay, reluctantly shares his story with his
fellow horses, which consider him to be a hero. Includes
factual information on bay horses.
    ISBN: 1-56763-647-0   (hc)
           1-56763-648-9 (pbk)

    1. Little Bighorn, Battle of the, Mont., 1876—Juvenile
fiction. [1. Little Bighorn, Battle of the, Mont., 1876—
Fiction. 2. Horses—Fiction. 3. Heroes—Fiction.]
I. Sargent, Pat, 1936- II. Lenoir, Jane, 1950- ill. III. Title.
IV. Series.

    PZ10.3. S243Com 2001
    [E]—dc21   2001-002982

Copyright © 2001 by Dave and Pat Sargent
All rights reserved

Printed in the United States of America

iv

Inspired by

seeing Comanche's preserved body that is on display at the University of Kansas. After he was wounded in the battle that has become known as "Custer's Last Stand," Comanche the red bay became America's most revered horse. He was not worked or ridden again. He died fifteen years later, at the age of twenty-nine, at Fort Riley, Kansas, in November 1891.

Dedicated to

all kids who love horses and heroes.

Foreword

Comanche, a courageous red bay, was proud to carry on his back General George Armstrong Custer. A big surprise was waiting for them when Comanche and General Custer, along with the 7th Cavalry and six hundred and fifty horses and their bosses, rode into the valley of the Little Big Horn River in Montana.

Almost immediately, arrows from three thousand Cheyenne and Sioux warriors began whizzing through the air. And when the battle was over, Comanche was the only survivor, horse or soldier, that was left standing, but the Indians were aiming their arrows straight for him. After taking many arrows, his world went black and he fell to the ground.

Contents

ix

Comanche

If you would like to have the authors of the Saddle Up Series visit your school, free of charge, call 1-800-321-5671 or 1-800-960-3876.

One

Comanche the Hero

The long banner above the front gate of the Rocking S Horse Ranch fluttered with the gentle breeze. It proclaimed, "WELCOME HOME, COMANCHE," in bright red letters. Small white clouds drifted lazily within the clear blue sky, and birds sang a salute to the exciting day. Everyone on the Rocking S Horse Ranch stood at attention as a cavalry soldier led a limping and very tired red bay horse up the lane toward the main ranch house.

The injured horse was saddled, but the soldier walked beside him. The stirrups of the cavalry saddle swung limply with each step.

A regiment of cavalry soldiers on horseback followed immediately behind them.

Comanche suddenly stopped and gazed at the scene. Hmmm, he thought. It looks like these folks are getting ready for a party. I wonder what the occasion is and who it's for.

"Come on, Comanche," the cavalry soldier said quietly. "These folks are waiting to meet the guest of honor."

Comanche looked around, but he didn't see anyone except for the regiment of the 7th Cavalry behind him.

"I'm speaking of you. Why, you are a national hero, Comanche," the soldier said with a chuckle.

"Me?" the red bay asked in a shocked voice. "Why me, Boss? I'm just a broken-down old cavalry horse."

The soldier just grinned and

patted him. As they walked a few more paces toward the crowd, a small boy ran to meet them.

"I love you, Comanche!" he yelled. "I'm going to help you get well. You are my hero!"

The red bay nuzzled him on the cheek, and the crowd cheered.

"It doesn't take much to please these folks," Comanche said with a chuckle. "I'm not a hero, but I don't think I'll tell them. It's kind of nice to get all of this friendly attention."

The owner of the ranch walked up and shook hands with the soldier and stroked Comanche's neck for a moment before speaking.

"Welcome to the Rocking S," he said. "We will take extra good care of Comanche during his retirement. This amazing horse will have everything he wants and more."

"We know he will," the soldier agreed with a smile. "That's why we chose the Rocking S for him."

Moments later, the regiment of horses and soldiers lined up in front of Comanche. The haunting sound of a bugle echoed over the land as

everyone saluted him. Hidden
beneath his coat of hair, he blushed
with embarrassment and pride.

Later that evening as the folks ate and sang, Comanche visited with his new friends in the barn.

"Tell us the story, Comanche," the dappled black said.

"Yes, tell us." The dark buckskin and the silver grullo nickered.

"What story do you want to hear?" the red bay asked. "I've been with the Seventh Cavalry for quite a while, and I've seen a lot of action."

"The *big one*," the lobo dun said. "We want to hear about the one that made you a hero."

Comanche looked at each horse before clearing his throat to speak.

"You are speaking of the battle that was fought in the valley of the Little Bighorn." He sighed before adding, "That's the one I don't like to talk about."

"Please tell us the story, Comanche," the sorrel pleaded. "Whatever happened there is the very reason you arrived at the Rocking S a national hero."

"Humph," the red bay snorted. "I'm a hero because I'm the only survivor."

"Not true," the pink-skinned palomino said. "You are a hero because you are brave, strong, loyal, and determined." He glared at the red bay and growled, "Now quit stalling and tell us your story."

"You win," Comanche said with a chuckle. "But I will not tell you until tomorrow." He yawned and rubbed his nose on his knee. "I'm tired, and my war wounds are hurting a bit. Good night, my friends."

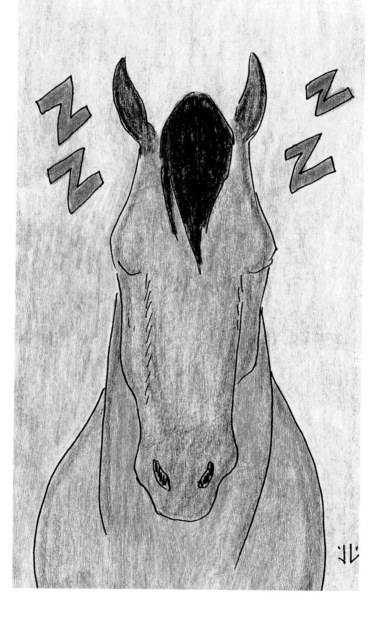

Two

Custer's Last Stand

The sun was peeking over the eastern horizon when the ranch hands arrived with oats and hay. After feeding all but Comanche, they left.

"Humph," the red bay said with a snort. "I don't feel too good about this hero stuff. It looks like I am going to miss a few meals!"

Suddenly the ranch hands returned with a special can of grain and a flake of green alfalfa hay. They headed straight for Comanche.

The red bay smiled and nodded his head as the sweet scent of molasses drifted into his nostrils from his manger.

"Oops," he said as he took a big bite from the center of the grain pile. "I better stop complaining and start appreciating, hadn't I?"

The other horses nickered in agreement as ranch hands brushed, curried, and doctored the wounds on the red bay. After tending to all of his wants and needs, they quietly left the barn.

"Now!" the dark buckskin said. "Now tell us the story of the battle in the valley of the Little Bighorn."

Comanche sighed and nodded his head. "Okay," he replied quietly. "General George Armstrong Custer was my boss. He was a dedicated and very determined military boss."

Comanche paused, and the smoky black quietly asked, "Is that the soldier who led you here?"

15

The red bay cleared his throat and said, "No. The day we went into the valley of the Little Bighorn changed everything. My boss and I were the leaders of six hundred and fifty of my horse friends and their soldier bosses. We found a large Indian village, and General Custer, who was my boss, decided to divide our regiment into four detachments. He gave each one of them a different mission. That left two hundred and fifty good horses, officers, and other soldiers to take care of the Indian village."

"It sounds like a workable plan," the dappled grey said quietly. "What happened then?"

"My boss didn't know it, but the village was full of fighting braves," the red bay said hoarsely.

"Savage Indians attacked us with bows and arrows and tomahawks. My boss and his soldiers had to leave us and fight the Indians on foot. The ground was much too rough for me and my friends to carry them through the battle. And then," Comanche added with a groan, "the Indians started aiming their arrows at me and my horse friends. I was hit many times with arrows before I went down, and everything went black . . . ."

As Comanche became silent, the barn was filled with sympathetic groans from the other horses. A full minute later, the red bay shook his head and said, "When I woke up sometime later, my boss and all of my friends and their bosses were dead. It was terrible!"

Again, Comanche paused for a moment, but not one horse in the barn broke the silence.

"I guess I stumbled away from the battlefield and Indian village," the red bay continued in a stronger voice. "Within hours, a detachment of horses and their bosses found me. They listened to my story and they doctored my wounds until I was able to come to the Rocking S."

Comanche looked around at his audience in the horse barn and a weak smile appeared on his lips.

"Now you should understand why I say that I am not a hero. I'm a survivor. That's all."

"No," the linebacked dun said quietly, "you are much more than a survivor, Comanche. You are the surviving hero."

Comanche smiled and slowly nodded his head.

"Okay, my friends, if you insist," the red bay agreed in a low voice. "I will be the surviving hero from the battle in Montana at the Little Bighorn River. But you must agree that we will never talk about it again."

"We'll never ask you to speak of it again, Comanche," the dappled grey said as he glared at the other horses.

"That's right," they all agreed. "We'll never speak of it again."

Three

The Golden Medallion

Later that morning, the ranch hands untied all but Comanche and led them from the barn. Each one of them protested.

"Why don't you take care of Comanche first?" one horse asked with a frown of disapproval.

But the ranch hands just shook their heads and ignored the horses.

"You'll understand later," one of the bosses said with a chuckle.

The sun was overhead when three soldiers entered the barn.

Hmmm, the red bay thought. Maybe it's my turn to be released into the corral. Good! I'm getting lonesome.

"Okay, Comanche," one of the soldiers said quietly. "It's time to get you ready."

"Me?" the red bay asked in a shocked voice. "Ready for what?"

The three cavalry soldiers carefully doctored Comanche's wounds before brushing and currying him to perfection. His mane and tail felt like soft silk, and his coat glistened from the detailed grooming. They put oil on his hooves and trimmed his fetlocks before stepping back to admire their work.

"Just look at you, Comanche," one of the soldiers muttered, "you look beautiful!"

"Humph," Comanche the red bay grumbled. "I bet I don't look like a loyal cavalry horse anymore. I probably look like a big sissy!"

Then the soldiers did something that startled him. His eyes were wide with surprise as they slipped his bridle over his head. They very carefully put the blanket and cavalry saddle on his back and tightened the cinch.

"Oh," Comanche said with a nod of his head. "Now I understand. You need for me to go back to work."

The red bay straightened his shoulders and held his head high as the soldiers led him from the barn.

"Okay, troops," he said in a husky voice. "My United States Cavalry needs me, and I am both

honored and happy to go back to
work."

The brightness of the sunlight momentarily hurt Comanche's eyes, and he blinked several times.

"Well now, what's all this?" he mumbled as he strained to see the usual regiment of horses and bosses lined up. "I must be dreaming. This sure doesn't look like regulation army duty!"

Suddenly a band started to play a happy tune, and a crowd of folks clapped and cheered. The soldier boss carefully led Comanche up the steps of a platform before turning him around to face the audience. The red bay stared in shocked silence as everyone stood up and cheered.

"W - w - w - what's happening, Boss?" he stuttered. "This is not the way to run the cavalry."

Suddenly the large crowd was silenced by a high-ranking officer.

"And now," the officer said, "we will hear a special message from the president of the United States, Ulysses S. Grant!"

Comanche felt his body go numb with shock. He shivered and shook his head. I must be dreaming again, he thought.

Moments later, the president slipped a red ribbon with a large golden medallion over his head. Then he deliberately cleared his throat and motioned to a soldier standing nearby. As the haunting sound of the bugle echoed throughout the countryside, every horse and every boss stood at attention and gave Comanche a respectful salute. The red bay did not realize that tears

of pride and joy were streaming
down his face.

"Okay, Boss. Enough of this," he said as he wiped the tears on one knee. "Let's go back to work."

The soldier grinned at the very surprised horse. Then he unbuckled the cinch and slid the cavalry saddle and blanket off Comanche's back.

"As the only survivor of Custer's Last Stand, Comanche," President Grant proclaimed, "you are hereby officially and honorably discharged from the United States Cavalry! May you enjoy your retirement years on the Rocking S Horse Ranch."

Hmmm, Comanche thought. This old red bay is being honored as the sole survivor of Custer's Last Stand at the Little Bighorn. But the real heroes are my horse friends and their bosses who died there. Well, it sounds like my life is smoothing out now and going to be worry free! Good. I'm ready.

Four

Red Bay Facts

The most common *bay* is the *red bay*. It is sometimes called a cherry bay. *Red bays* are a very clear red with little or no variation in intensity.

Bays are horses with black points and bodies that are colored some shade of red.

Bay is a very common color in horses, and *bays* come in several shades. There are *mahogany bays, seal brown bays, blood bays, sandy bays, and red bays.*

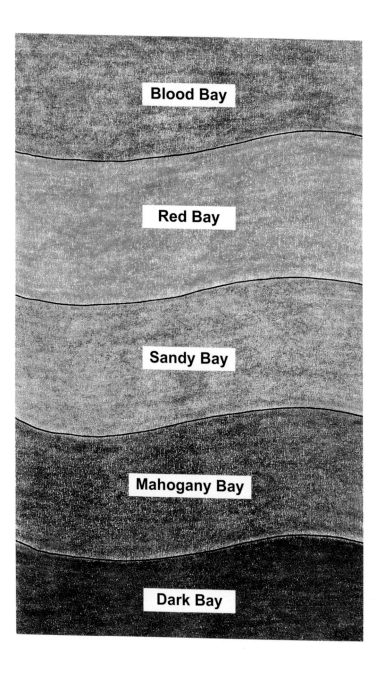